GROSSET & DUNLAP
Published by the Penguin Group
Penguin Group (USA) Inc., 375 Hudson Street, New York, New York 10014, USA
Penguin Group (Canada), 90 Eglinton Avenue East, Suite 700,
Toronto, Ontario M4P 2Y3, Canada
(a division of Pearson Penguin Canada Inc.)
Penguin Books Ltd., 80 Strand, London WC2R 0RL, England
Penguin Group Ireland, 25 St. Stephen's Green, Dublin 2, Ireland
(a division of Penguin Books Ltd.)
Penguin Group (Australia), 250 Camberwell Road, Camberwell, Victoria 3124, Australia
(a division of Pearson Australia Group Pty. Ltd.)
Penguin Books India Pvt. Ltd., 11 Community Centre, Panchsheel Park,
New Delhi—110 017, India
Penguin Group (NZ), 67 Apollo Drive, Rosedale, North Shore 0632, New Zealand
(a division of Pearson New Zealand Ltd.)
Penguin Books (South Africa) (Pty.) Ltd., 24 Sturdee Avenue,
Rosebank, Johannesburg 2196, South Africa

Penguin Books Ltd., Registered Offices:
80 Strand, London WC2R 0RL, England

Illustrated by Andrew Grey. Text by Laura Dollin.

Library of Congress Control Number: 2009036927

ISBN 978-0-448-45382-8   10 9 8 7 6 5 4 3 2 1

Grand
Adventures

Grosset & Dunlap
An Imprint of Penguin Group (USA) Inc.

The Search for a Heffalump

One sunny afternoon, when Winnie-the-Pooh,
Piglet, and Christopher Robin were enjoying
a friendly talk together, Christopher Robin
happened to say, "Piglet, I saw a Heffalump today."

Piglet felt a little uneasy, but wanted to sound as if he knew what Christopher Robin was talking about.

"I saw one once," Piglet replied. "At least, I think I did."

By and by, Piglet and Pooh decided it was time
to go home and walked side by side through
the Forest. After a moment, Pooh said solemnly,
"Piglet, I have decided something."

"What's that, Pooh?" asked Piglet.

"I have decided to catch a Heffalump,"
Pooh declared.

Piglet said nothing, but only because he rather wished he had come up with the idea first.

However, soon he forgot his disappointment and set about helping Pooh work out how to trap a Heffalump. It seemed that digging a **Very Deep Pit** would be a good start; a Deep Pit very near a Heffalump so that the Heffalump might fall into it quite quickly. Pooh and Piglet then wondered how one might keep the Heffalump there once trapped . . .

"Supposing you wanted to catch me," pondered Pooh. "How would you go about it?"

Piglet thought for a moment and then explained that he would make a Trap with honey inside it so that Pooh would smell the honey and go after it.

And so, before Pooh became too lost in his dreams of that sticky honey smell, Piglet sent him to fetch some honey while he set about digging the **Deep Pit**.

Pooh went home to find only one pot of honey left on his shelf. Surely he had some more?

Oh well, never mind. This will have to do, he thought.

A little while later, Pooh returned with a honey-pot. He passed it down to Piglet who was at the bottom of the Pit.

"Is that all you had left?" Piglet said, peering into the jar.

Pooh had to confess that he'd eaten some of the honey, just to make sure that it was honey and not anything else—cheese perhaps.

Piglet left the jar at the bottom of the Pit and the two friends said good night, agreeing to meet early the following morning to see how many Heffalumps they had caught in the Trap.

That night, Pooh woke up suddenly with a funny feeling in his tummy. He knew what that funny feeling meant—he was HUNGRY! So he went to the cupboard and reached up for a jar of honey. But he found NOTHING. Pooh was rather muddled and

walked back and forth, murmuring a murmur in a puzzled sort of way, before he remembered that he had put his last pot of honey into the Trap to catch a Heffalump.

"Bother!" he said, and went back to bed.

But Pooh couldn't
sleep and after trying
Counting Sheep, he
tried counting
Heffalumps.

But that
was no good,
either. He
jumped out
of bed and
ran straight
to the spot where the Very Deep Pit had
been dug.

There, at the bottom, was his jar of honey. And
although he had already eaten most of it, there
was a little left at the very bottom of the jar.

He pushed his head into the jar and began
to lick . . .

Meanwhile, Piglet woke up, his mind still a bit of a whirl with wonderings about Heffalumps like . . .

"What if Heffalumps don't like pigs very much?" and other such worrying thoughts.

He comforted himself with the knowledge that Pooh would be with him, but perhaps Heffalumps didn't like bears, either . . .

At sunrise, Piglet decided to be brave and check the Trap for Heffalumps. Off he went, muttering, "Oh dear, oh dear, oh dear!" as he did so. When he reached the Trap, he peered in.

At that moment, a loud roaring noise arose from the Pit. Piglet, as frightened as a little pig can be, scampered away.

"Help, help!" he cried. "A Herrible Hoffalump! Help! A Hoffable Hellerump!" And he didn't stop until he got to Christopher Robin's house.

"Whatever's the matter, Piglet?" asked Christopher Robin. Piglet explained about the Heffalump and how it had the biggest head you ever saw, like an enormous jar!

Christopher Robin agreed to come and look at it. He, too, could hear something as they got near the Pit. Then he began to laugh. And he laughed and laughed and laughed . . .

The terrible noise was Pooh, with his head
stuck in the jar,

against a tree root.

At that moment, Pooh's head popped out, and, on seeing Pooh Bear (not a Heffalump), Piglet realized what a silly animal he'd been.

He felt so very silly that he ran straight home to bed with a headache, while Christopher Robin and Pooh shared a loving chuckle before setting off to have breakfast together.

Piglet's Rainy Day

One morning, little Piglet looked out of his window and wished that he'd had Company all this time. For then, at least, he might have had a jolly time talking with Pooh or Christopher Robin about the rain. After all, it was quite exciting to see such a flood. But Piglet did feel a little Anxious.

"Pooh could escape by climbing trees," he thought. "Kanga could jump, Owl could fly . . . and here am I surrounded by water and I can't do anything."

Still it rained and rained, and every day the water got higher, until it was nearly up to Piglet's window. It was at this point that Piglet decided he should do something, and he **thought and thought** of what that something might be. Then he remembered that Christopher Robin had told him a story about a man on a desert island who wrote a message in a bottle before throwing it into the sea. That's what he would do! Then perhaps someone might find the bottle and come to rescue him.

So he found a bottle and some paper and a pencil, then he wrote:

before putting the paper in the bottle and corking the bottle tightly.

Piglet leaned out the window as far as he could without falling into the water and dropped the bottle with a *splash*! Watching it bob away into the distance, he hoped someone would find it very soon. Then he sighed a long sigh and wished that his friend Pooh was there because it was so very much more friendly with two.

Meanwhile, Pooh Bear woke up after a very long sleep to find his house was flooded and his feet were wet.

"This is Serious," he said to himself. And with that, he took his biggest pot of honey and escaped with it to a large branch of his tree.

Then he climbed down to get the next pot of honey, and the next one after that, and the next one after that . . . until his Escape was complete and Pooh was sitting on the branch with ten pots of honey beside him.

One jar at a time, Pooh ate all the honey. It was while enjoying the very last sticky mouthful that Pooh noticed Piglet's bottle floating past him. With only one thing on his mind, he plunged into the water with a loud cry of: "HONEY!"

But it soon became clear no honey was inside. "Bother!" said Pooh. Then he saw the piece of paper. He took it out and pondered upon it for a moment. "Hmmm," he said. "It's a Missage. That's what it is . . . and that letter is a *P* and *P* means 'Pooh.'" He decided to find Christopher Robin or Owl to help him read it.

Being a Bear who couldn't swim, Pooh realized he would have to find another way to get to them. An idea came to him, one he was rather pleased about (being a Bear of **Very Little Brain**) . . .

"If a bottle can float," he said to himself, "a jar can float, and if it's a big enough jar, I can sit on top of it."

So he took his biggest jar and made it watertight. Naming his newfound vessel the Floating Bear, he set off, bobbing **up** and **down** a bit, just managing to paddle through the rainwater.

It was just about this moment in time that, in another part of the Wood, Christopher Robin bumped into Owl. Together they were wondering whether Pooh and Piglet were all right in these rainy conditions. Just as Christopher Robin began to worry about his lovable Bear, a growly voice behind him said, "Hello, I'm here!"

Christopher Robin was so pleased to see Pooh that he gave him a huge hug.

Pooh proudly showed him his boat and then the Very Important Missage in the bottle.

"It's from Piglet!" cried Christopher Robin, reading the message. (It was then that Pooh realized the *P*s were for "Piglet" and not for "Pooh.")

"We must rescue him!" said Pooh.

With that, he sent Owl off to tell Piglet that Rescue was on its way.

By now, Piglet was beginning to think that perhaps he might never be rescued and that he would try hard to be very brave.

So he was most grateful to see Owl, when he arrived to tell him of the coming Rescue.

Although the Rescue didn't come soon enough for poor Piglet, who had to listen to Owl's very long story about an aunt who laid a seagull's egg by mistake.

Feeling very tired, Piglet began to fall asleep and it was only a loud

SQUAWK!

from Owl that woke him with a start and stopped him from falling out the window and into the water.

You can therefore imagine Piglet's joy and relief when he saw Christopher Robin and Pooh floating toward him in an umbrella! (Pooh had astounded even Christopher Robin with his clever umbrella idea.)

At last, Piglet was being rescued! Once again, he could be with his dearest friend, Pooh Bear, and enjoy some Company.

And that is the end of Piglet's Big Adventure in the rain—an adventure in which, I think you'll agree, he was a **Very Brave Piglet**.